DUCK at the DOOR

Jackie Urbanovic

HarperCollinsPublishers

Duck at the Door
Copyright © 2007 by Jackie Urbanovic

Manufactured in China.
All rights reserved. No part of this book may be used or reproduced in any
manner whatsoever without written permission except in the case of brief
quotations embodied in critical articles and reviews.
For information address HarperCollins Children's Books, a division of
HarperCollins Publishers,
1350 Avenue of the Americas, New York, NY 10019.
www.harpercollinschildrens.com

Library of Congress Cataloging-in-Publication Data is available.
ISBN-10: 0-06-121438-8 (trade bdg.) — ISBN-13: 978-0-06-121438-7 (trade bdg.)
ISBN-10: 0-06-121439-6 (lib. bdg.) — ISBN-13: 978-0-06-121439-4 (lib. bdg.)

Typography by Carla Weise
1 2 3 4 5 6 7 8 9 10
❖
First Edition

This special edition created for Kohl's ISBN 978-0-06-179142-0

For Susan Dreiband,
my behind-the-scenes co-creator.

With thanks to Jane Resh Thomas, who taught me to write, and to
her writing group for so much laughter and support. To Max Haynes,
who was always willing to share his time and ideas. And, of course,
to the real Irene, Brody, and Scrappy, who inspired this story.

It was a quiet
night until . . .

Thunk, creak, and KNOCK, KNOCK, KNOCK!

SOMEONE IS OUT THERE!

BUT WHO?

"LET'S GO ASK IRENE!

SHE ALWAYS KNOWS WHAT TO DO."

"Irene!" cried Brody. "Help!
Someone is knocking on our door!"

"It's the middle of the night," said Irene.
"Who could be knocking on our door?"

It's a
DUCK!

Irene brought the duck inside.

"My name is Max," he began. "I was born in the spring, and I loved it. I stayed behind when my flock flew south because I thought I'd love winter too. But it turned out to be COLD and very lonely."

"Winter isn't so bad when you have a warm home," said Irene.

At first Max
had a lot to learn.

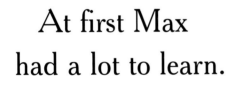

In January he learned to use the remote control.
(He enjoyed *Wild Kingdom* and *World Wide Wrestling*.)

In February he
discovered he had
a flair for cooking.

By March he had made
himself right at home.

But by April it was clear that Max had learned too much.

Dakota, Coco, and Jesse Bear
got tired of Max's new recipes.

Max's Tofu Surprise!

Shish Kebob à la Max

Max's Seaweed Chowder

And Brody
was just tired.

Someone had to talk to Max.

But **WHO**?

Just then Max burst into the room yelling, "Listen to the quacking! My flock has returned! I can't wait to see them."

"Irene, please keep my chef's hat. And Brody, you can have my rubber duckies. I will miss you all so much!"

After many hugs, Max left.

With Max gone, life was ordinary again.

You go first.

No, you.

The cats went back to
eating plain cat food.

No one played keep-away
with the remote control.

What else can
we do for fun?

And Brody didn't have to share his bed.

Life was so quiet that by October, everyone
was happy to hear the sound of quacking.
When there was a knock at the door, everyone
was hoping the same thing.

"MAX!" they shouted with joy.
"Are you staying with us all winter?"
they asked.

"Yes," said Max. "Me and . . .

...MY FLOCK!"

Everyone looked at Irene, hoping she would say something.

But all she could say was

"WELCOME HOME!"